Morgan the Midnight Fairy

For Ruby Barron, with lots of love

Special thanks to Sue Mongredien

ISBN 978-0-545-27047-2

Previously published as Twilight Fairies #4: *Morgan the Midnight Fairy* by Orchard U.K. in 2010.

All rights reserved. Published by Scholastic Inc., 557 Broadway, New York, NY 10012, by arrangement with Rainbow Magic Limited.

12 11 10 9 8 7 6 5 4 3 2   11 12 13 14 15/0

Printed in the U.S.A.   40

First Scholastic Printing, July 2011

Morgan
the Midnight
Fairy

by Daisy Meadows

SCHOLASTIC INC.

New York   Toronto   London   Auckland

Sydney   Mexico City   New Delhi   Hong Kong

The Fairyland Palace

Observatory

Game
A

Fairy Homes

Ferry

CAMP STARGAZE

Mirror Lake

The Twinkling Tree

Starry Glade

The Night Fairies' special magic powers
Bring harmony to the nighttime hours.
But now their magic belongs to me,
And I'll cause chaos, you shall see!

In sunset, moonlight, and starlight, too,
There'll be no more sweet dreams for you.
From evening dusk to morning light,
I am the master of the night!

Contents

The Midnight Hour

"I'm not tired at all. Are you?" Kirsty Tate asked her best friend, Rachel Walker. It was late at night, and the two girls were in the Whispering Woods, shining their flashlights into the shadows as they collected firewood. They were staying with their families at a vacation spot called Camp Stargaze. Tonight, the whole camp was having a midnight feast.

"Not one bit," Rachel replied as she tugged at a branch from the undergrowth. "I'm too excited to even think about being tired!" She grinned at Kirsty. "What a great vacation this is turning out to be. A whole week

together, lots of adventures, a midnight feast, and . . ." She lowered her voice, cautiously glancing around. "And plenty of fairy magic, too!"

Kirsty smiled. It was true—she and Rachel had been having a wonderful time this week.

On their very first evening in camp, they'd met Ava the Sunset Fairy, who was one of seven Night Fairies. The Night Fairies looked after the world between dusk and dawn, making sure that everything stayed peaceful and happy with the help of their special bags of magic dust. But a few nights ago,

Jack Frost had stolen these bags while the seven fairies were having a party. Luckily, Kirsty and Rachel were friends with the fairies! They'd had lots of exciting adventures with them before, so when the Night Fairies asked if they would help search for the stolen fairy dust, Kirsty and Rachel were happy to say yes.

So far they had found three bags of magic dust belonging to Ava the Sunset

Fairy, Lexi the Firefly Fairy, and Zara the Starlight Fairy, but there were still four left to find.

It was a chilly night, and Kirsty and Rachel were happy to see that the moon and stars were shining brightly. "Zara's starlight magic is working perfectly again," Kirsty said, gazing up at the twinkling stars. She gathered some more sticks, humming cheerfully to herself.

Tonight was going to be so much fun! Peter, one of the camp counselors, was lighting a big fire, and then there were

going to be lots of fireworks at the stroke
of midnight, followed by a feast for
everyone.

As the girls made their way through
the dark woods, they heard a voice
calling: "Kirsty, Rachel, is that you?
We've found lots of firewood down
here!"

"Follow the beam of our flashlights!"

shouted a second
voice. Then the girls
saw bright white
beams of light
flashing through the
trees in the distance.

"Sounds like Lucas
and Matt," Rachel said. "Come on, let's
find them."

"We're on our way!" Kirsty called. She and Rachel had become good friends with Lucas and Matt while they'd been at camp. They had all had a lot of fun together so far.

Before long, Rachel and Kirsty saw a grove ahead, with Lucas and Matt standing in the middle, still waving their flashlights around.

"Be careful," Matt warned. "The path is a little slippery, so—"

Just as he said the words, Rachel felt
her foot skid on some pine needles on the
path. She grabbed Kirsty to try to keep
her balance but couldn't help slipping.
"*Whoa!*" she yelled as she completely
lost her footing and fell on her bottom.
She accidentally pulled Kirsty down, too.
They both dropped their firewood as
they slipped and slid down into the grove
with a bump-bump-BUMP!

Luckily, they landed on soft patches of moss and weren't hurt. Lucas and Matt helped them up, then they all started gathering the dropped firewood together.

"It's pretty down here, isn't it?" Kirsty said, shining her flashlight around. The glade was circular, with tall pine trees around it. As she swung the beam along the ground, she saw that there were hundreds of tiny, white, star-shaped flowers dotting the velvety, green moss.

"It's called Starry Glade," Matt told them. "Because of those star-shaped flowers, I guess. Or maybe because when you look up at night, all you can see are the stars."

"And fireworks, too, tonight," Lucas reminded him. "Come on, let's take this firewood back. It can't be too long until midnight!"

Sparks Fly!

Rachel, Kirsty, Lucas, and Matt headed back to the large clearing where the other campers had gathered. The adults were preparing the campfire for the midnight feast and had built a large pile of sticks, surrounded by a ring of stones.

"Kids, make sure you stay outside of the stone ring," Peter the camp counselor told them. "Once we get the fire blazing, it's going to be very hot, and sparks might fly." He patted his pockets. "Speaking of lighting the fire, I'd better get started. Where did I put those matches?"

Kirsty and Rachel set their firewood on a pile close by while Peter kept searching for the matches. "I'm sure I packed them," he muttered, rifling through his backpack. "Where are they?"

Kirsty's dad grabbed a couple of dry sticks. "I wasn't in the Outdoor Adventurers for nothing," he said, rubbing them together. "I'll have a spark in a minute, and we can get that fire going."

Unfortunately, no spark appeared even though Mr. Tate kept trying. Peter still couldn't find his matches. A few minutes later, Rachel's parents came into the clearing carrying boxes of food for the feast.

"Oh!" said Mrs. Walker in surprise. "I thought the fire would be lit by now. We'll have to hurry if we're going to cook these hot dogs by midnight."

Rachel explained the problem, and her mom smiled. "Don't worry," she said, "I have some matches in my emergency kit. Let me see. . . . Here!"

Everyone broke into applause as Mrs. Walker triumphantly held up the matchbox. Peter wasted no time in striking a match and getting the fire to light.

Kirsty and Rachel sat on a nearby log to watch. Despite the huge mountain of firewood that had been collected, the fire stayed disappointingly small.

The flames crawled along the twigs but didn't catch on any of the larger branches. Smoke billowed into the air, making people cough and choke.

"Let's get cooking," Mr. Walker said, loading up a pan with hot dogs and onions and balancing it on the fire. He winked at Rachel and Kirsty. "You can't beat the smell of hot dogs sizzling on a campfire, that's what I always say!"

But unfortunately, even after a long time, the hot dogs were not sizzling and still looked pink and raw. "They don't seem to be cooking at all." Mr. Walker frowned. "I don't think the fire is hot enough."

"Should we try toasting the marshmallows instead?" Kirsty suggested, feeling hungry. She and Rachel had found some special long, thin sticks that looked especially good for marshmallow-toasting.

"Great idea," Mrs. Tate said, opening

the marshmallow bags and passing them around. Everyone popped marshmallows onto their sticks before carefully holding them in the campfire.

"I love the way the outsides get crunchy, but the insides are warm and gooey," Rachel said, watching her marshmallow as the flames flickered around it. "But remember, you shouldn't

leave it in too long. Burnt marshmallows are not very tasty!"

"No," Kirsty agreed. "The second it turns brown, you need to pull it out of the fire—and gobble it up!"

The girls waited and waited for their marshmallows to toast, but they stayed white for a long time. "They have to be ready by now," Rachel said, taking hers out of the fire and cautiously testing it against her lips. "Oh," she said in surprise. "It's still cold!"

Kirsty tried hers, and so did the other campers. Their marshmallows were cold, too! What was going on? Why wasn't the fire cooking anything?

"The Midnight Feast is going to be a midnight flop at this rate," Mr. Tate said in dismay. People nearby were muttering grumpily about feeling tired and wanting to go to bed. "Maybe this wasn't such a good idea after all."

Just then, the fire crackled loudly as a log split right down the middle, and glowing sparks flew up into the dark sky. Everybody backed off, including Rachel and Kirsty. No one wanted to be burned by a hot spark.

As they stepped away from the fire, the girls saw that one of the sparks seemed to be headed straight for them. They dodged to the side, and the spark flew into the darkness and vanished. As it passed them, Kirsty noticed that the "spark" had shimmering silver wings.

"That's no spark," she whispered to
Rachel. "It's Morgan the Midnight
Fairy!"

A Spooky Story

Kirsty and Rachel had met all seven of the Night Fairies on the first day of their adventure. They felt very excited as they slipped away from the campfire in the direction Morgan had flown. "There she is, on that tree stump!" Rachel whispered, hurrying toward the little fairy.

Morgan waved and fluttered into the
air as the girls
approached.
She had blond
hair in a sweet
pixie style, with a
midnight-blue
headband. She wore a
pretty, dark blue dress
with matching sparkly,
peep-toe shoes.

Rachel quickly opened her coat pocket
so Morgan could fly inside and avoid
being seen by anyone else. She and
Kirsty still had their backs to the fire,
so they could talk to Morgan in secret.
"Hello," Rachel whispered. "Nice to see
you again!"

"You, too," Morgan replied. "But I'm

sorry the midnight feast isn't going well. As the Midnight Fairy, I can usually make midnight feasts and parties really exciting, with the help of my magic night dust. Ever since Jack Frost stole it, midnight parties have been going wrong all over the world—in Fairyland, too."

Kirsty nodded. "Our fire won't light well, and it isn't cooking the food. People are getting really frustrated. They're even talking about going to bed."

"And that would be a real shame, because we've got fireworks planned for midnight," Rachel added.

Morgan looked anxious. "Then I really have to find my night dust before then," she said. "If I don't, I'm sure that the fireworks will be a total letdown."

Just then, Peter clapped his hands loudly. "OK, everyone! Listen up," he called, smiling. Kirsty and Rachel turned back to see that the sparks from the campfire had died away. Everyone was sitting on logs around the fire again. Kirsty and Rachel sat down quickly, too.

"To get everyone in a spooky mood for midnight, we'll go around the circle, taking turns telling part of a ghost story," Peter explained. "I'll start things off." He cleared his throat.

"Once upon a time, it was a dark, stormy night, and two children were

lost in the woods. . . ."

Rachel shivered with delight. She loved
ghost stories! But as the story passed
around the circle, it became more silly
than spooky.

". . . And they met a giant . . . sheep,"
a boy named Jake said with a giggle.
"And the sheep gave a big sneeze, and
all its wool fell off onto the kid's heads!"

Jake's big sister, Laura, made a face. "Jake! Don't fool around," she told him. "Tell the story correctly."

Jake shrugged. "That's all I can think of," he replied. "I'm too tired to make up a story, anyway."

"We're all tired and cold, but there's no reason to—" Laura began arguing.

"OK, OK," Peter interrupted quickly. "Let's not argue. A giant sheep is fine. Kirsty, do you want to add some of the story? What happens next?"

"Um . . ." Kirsty said. "The kids pulled the sheep's wool off their heads and went farther into the forest," she said, thinking fast. "Then something really scary happened."

"What?" Lucas interrupted.

"They saw . . ." Kirsty's mind went

blank. She had no idea what could happen next! She tried to think of the most terrifying thing she'd ever seen in her life. Then, before she could stop herself, she blurted out, "The children saw JACK FROST!"

Rachel gasped. "Kirsty!" she hissed in a warning tone. She and Kirsty were supposed to keep their fairy adventures secret. No other humans were supposed to know about Fairyland or the

magical creatures who lived there. And that included Jack Frost!

Kirsty clapped a hand over her mouth. "Sorry," she whispered. "It just came out."

Thankfully, just then, Matt gave a cry. "There's a monster!" he yelled, pointing into the shadowy bushes with a shaking finger. "I saw a monster running over there. It had a long nose and big feet, and it was g-g-g-green!"

Peter laughed. Rachel could tell Peter thought Matt was joking and that this was all part of the story. Some of the other grown-ups laughed, too. "There are no such things as monsters!" Matt's mom told him. "It's just your imagination."

But Kirsty and Rachel didn't laugh—they looked at each other with concern. They were sure that the green thing Matt had described wasn't a monster, or "just his imagination." It had to be one of Jack Frost's sneaky goblins!

Gobbling Goblins

"Should we get some more firewood?" Rachel asked, standing. "I think I need to stretch my legs."

"Me, too," Kirsty said, standing up beside her. Like Rachel, she was eager to find out what the goblin was doing in the Whispering Woods. Goblins were tricky creatures, and the girls were sure that the one Matt saw had to be up to no good!

"OK," Rachel's dad said. "Watch out for monsters, though," he joked.

Kirsty and Rachel set off in the direction that Matt had pointed when he saw the monster. Once they were safely hidden by the trees, Morgan fluttered out of Rachel's pocket. "That was a goblin your friend spotted," she told them. "I saw him myself, and it looked like he was in a real hurry. I wonder what's going on." She took out her wand.

"Let's fly deeper into the woods and see if we can find him."

When Morgan waved her wand

over the girls, a stream of fairy magic
swirled out of it. The dust glittered with
tiny golden clock shapes. As the magic
tumbled around Kirsty and Rachel, they
felt themselves
shrinking smaller
and smaller,
until they were
the same size
as Morgan.
They both had
their very own
pair of sparkling
fairy wings. With a
few quick flutters, they were up
in the air, as high as the treetops.

   The woods were bathed in silver
moonlight and looked wonderfully
magical, Kirsty thought as she flew.

An owl hooted softly somewhere close by, and the leaves rustled in the trees below.

Soon they heard footsteps, and Rachel pointed downward. "There he is!" she said. The goblin was skipping along happily. They stayed behind him and followed him through the trees. It wasn't long before they could smell the delicious aroma of food cooking and hear cheerful singing.

The goblin led them all the way to a clearing where a whole gang of other goblins were sitting around a campfire, about to have their own midnight feast. This was a happier feast than the one Rachel and Kirsty had just left! The fire blazed, and the goblins who weren't singing were biting into hot dogs and baked potatoes cooked by the heat of the flames.

"Delicious," one goblin said, cramming the rest of his hot dog into his mouth and chewing hard. Crumbs sprayed everywhere, and Rachel and Kirsty made faces at each other. *Yuck!*

"And what I crave now," said the same goblin as he picked up a dark-blue satin bag and opened the drawstrings, "is some bogmallows. Give me bogmallows!"

Morgan gasped. "That's my bag of magic night dust!" she whispered to Kirsty and Rachel.

They watched as the goblin plunged his hand into the satin bag and took out a pinch of sparkling dust. He sprinkled the dust into the air. Then, with a shimmering light, a large pile of green marshmallows appeared next to him.

Rachel and Kirsty had seen green marshmallows before when they had helped Gabriella the Snow Kingdom Fairy on another adventure. They knew that they were a kind of goblin treat called "bogmallows."

The goblin whooped. "Woo-hoo! Bogmallows, everyone! Come and get them!"

He reached into the bag and sprinkled more fairy dust. Another large pile of bogmallows appeared. The goblins

crowded around with big sticks, shoving the bogmallows on three at a time before toasting them.

"Wow," Kirsty said. "That's a lot of bogmallows!"

"And a waste of magic dust," Morgan added angrily. "We've got to get my bag back, before he uses it all up!"

"Give me a try with that dust," another goblin with a squeaky voice said as he grabbed at the bag. "I want to use the magic to make more hot dogs."

"No!" the first goblin said, jerking the bag out of reach. "You already had lots of hot dogs. Don't be greedy."

"I'm thirsty," a third goblin complained. He tried to grab the bag, too. "Give me that, and I'll make some more soda with the special magic."

"No!" the first goblin said again. "It's mine and you're not getting it." Then

he put the bag
on the log and
quickly sat on top
of it, so the bag was
completely covered
by his bottom.

Rachel groaned.
"How are we going to
get the bag now?" she wondered
anxiously. "Quick—we've got to think
of a plan!"

BOO!

"We need to get him off that log," Kirsty said, thinking aloud. "Maybe if he saw something exciting — or scary! — he would jump to his feet. *Hmmm . . .*"

"I've got it!" Rachel exclaimed. "We can frighten him out of his seat . . . by telling him a ghost story!"

"That's a great idea," Morgan said. "But, wait! If we fly in like this, the goblins will know we're trying to get my bag back. We need some disguises."

"Could you use your magic to make me look like a goblin?" Kirsty suggested. "Then I could sit down with them and tell them a spooky story."

"Yes," said Rachel. Her words tumbled out enthusiastically as she thought of something else. "And maybe if I'm disguised as a ghost, I could pop out when you get to the scariest part, Kirsty—and I'll make all the goblins jump!"

The three friends grinned at one another. "Perfect," Morgan said. They flew down and landed behind a thick bush so she could work some fairy magic without being seen. She waved her wand, and once again, a stream of glittery sparkles swirled out and floated around Kirsty and Rachel. Moments later, Kirsty felt her nose and ears becoming much bigger and more pointy.

Rachel giggled. "You look just like a goblin!" she said.

Kirsty's eyes grew wide as she saw Rachel. "Is that really you?" she gasped. "You look so scary!"

Rachel had turned into a ghostly figure—a shapeless, white, gleaming ghost, with dark, hollow eyes and a sad mouth. "Good," she replied. "Let's go and scare those goblins!"

"Try to do it quickly," Morgan advised. "These disguises use up a lot of magic. They won't last very long. Good luck!"

Rachel hid behind a tree and watched Kirsty join the goblin group. Kirsty tried to look as casual as possible, but her heart was pounding fast. She was next to the goblin who was sitting on the bag of magic dust! "Time for a ghost story!" she announced. "Is everyone listening?"

The goblins seemed happy to hear a story, and they sat down quickly, all eyes on Kirsty.

"Once upon a time . . ." Kirsty began in a low, spooky voice. She told them a story about a haunted house where ghostly pogwurzels lurked—goblins were very scared of pogwurzels! It wasn't long before her audience was shivering and clutching at one another for comfort.

"The goblin creeped through the house," Kirsty went on, dropping her voice even lower. "And then, all of a sudden . . ."

"*BOO!*" shouted Rachel, leaping out from behind the tree.

"*Aarrrrrghhh!*" screamed the goblins, all jumping up in fright. "Help!"

This was Morgan's cue to swoop in

and grab her bag of magic dust. But, just then, one of the goblins pointed at Rachel. "Hey! That's not a ghost—it's a pesky girl!" he shouted.

Kirsty gulped. Oh, no! Rachel's magic disguise was wearing off. When she glanced down at herself, she realized hers was, too! "Quick, Morgan!" she called out—but she was too late. The goblin who'd been sitting on the bag whirled around and grabbed it before Morgan could reach it. He rushed out of the campfire ring, followed by the rest of his gang.

Morgan waved her wand and turned

Kirsty and Rachel back into fairies.
"After them!" she called. "Come on!"

The three fairies soared after the racing
goblins, who were charging through the
dark woods at top speed. Rachel, Kirsty,
and Morgan soon spotted the goblin
with the bag right at the front of the
pack. He glanced over his shoulder, and
a nervous look
came over his face
as he saw the
three fairies
flying behind
him. "Here—
take this!" he
shouted, tossing
the bag of
magic dust to one
of his friends.

The other goblin caught the bag, but just as Rachel, Kirsty, and Morgan headed toward him, he threw it to another goblin, who caught it and kept running.

The chase went on through the woods with the goblins throwing the bag to one another. The fairies became more and more frustrated as they swerved from goblin to goblin, trying to keep up! Dry sticks and leaves snapped beneath the goblins' big, flat feet as they thudded between the tall trees.

Rachel was beginning to worry. How were they going to get Morgan's bag back from so many goblins? Then she noticed the stars that were twinkling in the night sky. They reminded her of all the tiny white flowers she and Kirsty had seen in Starry Glade earlier that evening. It seemed like ages since the two of them had slid down the hill there.

"Wait!" she whispered to Kirsty and Morgan as an idea popped into her head. "I just thought of something! Remember how we fell down that steep slope into Starry Glade earlier?" Kirsty nodded. "Well, if we could lead the goblins that same way, maybe they

will slip down the hill, just like we did,"
Rachel went on. "And if they do . . ."

"We can fly in
and grab my bag
of night dust!"
Morgan finished
with a smile. "I
know the glade you
mean, and we're not far away.
Come on, let's see if your plan works."

The fairies caught up with the goblins
as they raced along. Every time the path
forked, Morgan would zip ahead and
hover at the start of the path they didn't
want the goblins to take. "Give me my
bag!" she'd call, with her hands on her
hips.

"No way!" the goblins would yell,
always turning down the other path.

Then Kirsty, Rachel, and Morgan would high-five each other in secret. This was just what they wanted!

Eventually, they steered the goblins onto the path that ran down to Starry Glade. Kirsty, Rachel, and Morgan raced over their heads. "I can see the bag!" Kirsty cried loudly. "Let's get it!"

The goblin carrying the bag panicked and glanced around for someone to throw it to.

But as he looked away from the path,
he slipped on the pine needles — and let
go of Morgan's bag. It went flying into
the air!

Feast of Fun

Rachel and Kirsty raced toward the bag, while Morgan used her magic to turn it to its usual Fairyland size. "Caught it!" cheered Kirsty, as she grabbed hold of the satiny material. She then flew up high with it in her hands.

Below them, the goblins were slipping
and sliding and falling over one another
in a tangle of arms and legs. Kirsty and
Rachel smiled as Morgan flew over to
join them. "Oh, good job!" Morgan
exclaimed, taking the bag and hugging
both Kirsty and
Rachel. "And
just in time—
it's almost
midnight!"
She grinned.
"Come on, let's
leave these goblins
here and hurry back to
your camp's midnight feast. We might
be able to turn it into a night full of fun
after all!" She took out a pinch of her
night dust and muttered some magic

words that sent the sparkly gold dust
spiraling into the trees. "There," she
said. "That's a start. Let's see what's
happening now."

The three friends flapped their wings
and set off through the dark woods
again. As they got near the clearing
where their feast was taking place, a
yummy smell drifted up to them.

"*Mmmm* . . . They've got the hot dogs
cooking!" Rachel realized, with a big
grin.

"And look—you can see the campfire
from here!" Kirsty exclaimed, pointing
ahead to where bright flames were
blazing. The twigs crackled and snapped.

Morgan smiled. "I'll turn you back
into girls, so you can join your friends
and family," she said, waving her wand.

In the next moment, Kirsty and Rachel felt themselves growing all the way back to their usual sizes, with their feet firmly on the ground again. "Now, you were supposed to be collecting more firewood,

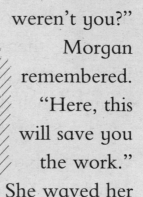

weren't you?" Morgan remembered. "Here, this will save you the work." She waved her wand again, and a pile of dry sticks and branches appeared in both Rachel's and Kirsty's arms. "Perfect for the fire!" Morgan smiled. Then she kissed each girl on the cheek and waved good-bye. "I'd better fly around and make sure that all the other midnight feasts are going as well as yours," she told them. "Thanks again—oh, and watch for a big surprise!"

Before the girls could ask what she meant, Morgan had vanished.

Kirsty and Rachel dumped their firewood in a pile near Peter, and went back to their places at the campfire. "Marshmallows, girls?" Mrs. Tate asked, offering them the bag.

"Yes, please!" they replied eagerly.

The rest of the midnight feast was lots

of fun. Everyone enjoyed toasting (and eating!) the sweet, gooey marshmallows,

as well as devouring the hot dogs, potatoes, and chili. There was even time for a campfire singalong before the midnight fireworks!

"Oooh!" *"Ahhhh!"* Everyone sighed as bright flashes of color glittered and glowed against the midnight sky. And then, just as Kirsty and Rachel thought the night couldn't get any more perfect, the last set of fireworks went off with an extraordinary series of bangs. Some sparkly writing appeared in the sky.

"Enjoy the Midnight Magic!" Peter read aloud in surprise.

"Wow! How did that happen?" someone asked.

Peter looked baffled. "I have no idea," he confessed, scratching his head. Rachel and Kirsty grinned at each other. They knew that Morgan must have "helped" the fireworks with some of her magic. But that, of course, was going to stay their very special secret!

RAINBOW magic

THE NIGHT FAIRIES

Rachel and Kirsty have helped Morgan,
and now it's time to lend a hand to

Nia
the Night Owl Fairy!

Join their next nighttime adventure
in this special sneak peek. . . .

Night or Day?

"Hold on tight, Kirsty," Rachel called to her best friend, Kirsty Tate. "We're almost there!"

"I'm right behind you, Rachel!" Kirsty called back.

The girls were walking carefully across the wobbly bridge in the Forest Fun

Adventure Playground. The wooden bridge was part of a high-ropes course. It was strung between two trees way above the ground. It swayed and wobbled gently as the girls moved across it, making them shriek with laughter.

"Oh, this is too much fun!" Kirsty gasped. "I love Camp Stargaze, Rachel. There's so much to do here."

The girls and their parents were spending a week of summer vacation at Camp Stargaze, and the Forest Fun playground was in a clearing in the woods on the edge of the campground. There was a treetop walk, a few hideouts, and two ziplines next to each other, as well as the wobbly bridge. The biggest tree in the clearing, the one the girls were heading toward on the wobbly bridge, had a wooden treehouse in its branches. There was also a twisty slide that wrapped around the tree's trunk and led down to an underground fort built below the roots of the tree.

It was late afternoon, just after snack time, and the girls were still enjoying the warmth of the summer sun.

"I know," Rachel agreed. "Camp Stargaze is amazing. And not only that, we're in the middle of another exciting fairy adventure, too!"

"Rachel, Kirsty!" a voice shouted. "We're over here."

The girls glanced up and saw their new friends Matt and Lucas hanging out of one of the treehouse windows. Rachel and Kirsty wobbled to the end of the bridge and went to join them inside the treehouse.

"Have you been on the ziplines yet?" Lucas asked with a grin.

Kirsty shook her head. "I think I need to recover from the wobbly bridge first!" she replied.

Matt was still hanging out of the window. "Look, Lucas," he said, pointing down at the ground below them. "There's your mom and Lizzy."

Lucas's mom and his little sister were wandering through the clearing. They waved up at the treehouse, and Lucas, Rachel, Kirsty, and Matt waved back.

"Let's go down the twisty slide and say hi!" Rachel suggested.

The top of the silver slide was just outside the treehouse door. Rachel climbed onto it and then immediately shot down with a shriek of surprise.

"It's really slippery!" she cried as she disappeared from view.

"Watch out, Rachel!" Kirsty yelled as she jumped on the slide, too. "Here I come!"

Laughing, Rachel zoomed around the trunk of the tree, then through the trapdoor the underground house at the bottom. She tumbled off the end of the slide and onto a soft cushion. Kirsty came flying into the underground house a few seconds later, and the two girls grinned at each other.

"Here come the boys!" Rachel said as they heard Matt and Lucas sliding toward them.

First Matt, and then Lucas, tumbled

into the underground house. Next, all
four of them climbed out and ran to
join Lucas's mom and Lizzy. They were
staring very closely at a large, leafy bush.

"What are you looking at?" Lucas
asked curiously.

"Porcupines," Lucas's mom replied.
Both her and Lizzy's eyes were wide with
delight. "Look!"

Rachel and Kirsty peeked into the
bush, and saw two small porcupines
scampering around in the leaves.

"Aren't they cute?" said Rachel as the
porcupines scurried back and forth.

Just then, Kirsty heard a rustling noise
in the undergrowth behind them. She
spun around and caught a glimpse of
gray fur and a black-and-white striped
head. Quickly, she nudged Rachel.

"There's a badger over there!" Kirsty whispered.

Rachel, Lucas, and the others watched in amazement as the badger came into view. He was sniffing through the leaves in search of something to eat.

"This is great!" Matt said, looking excited as the badger hurried past, not even noticing them. "I've never seen a badger or a porcupine during the day before."

Kirsty frowned. "Matt's right," she said to Rachel. "Don't porcupines and badgers usually come out at night?"

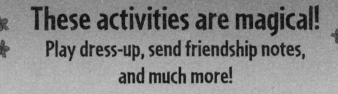

These activities are magical!
Play dress-up, send friendship notes, and much more!

SCHOLASTIC
www.scholastic.com
www.rainbowmagiconline.com

RMACT